HOGWARTS LIBRARY

Title:	Quidditch Through the Ages
Author:	Kennilworthy Whisp

Date Due	Name
08 JAN	R. Weasley stinks **OVERDUE**

THIS BOOK IS THE PROPERTY OF

DRACO DORMIENS NUNQUAM TITILLANDUS

HOGWARTS LIBRARY

QUIDDITCH
THROUGH
THE AGES

Praise for
QUIDDITCH
THROUGH THE AGES

'Kennilworthy Whisp's painstaking research has uncovered a veritable treasure trove of hitherto unknown facts about the sport of warlocks. A fascinating read.'

Bathilda Bagshot, author, *A History of Magic*

'Whisp has produced a thoroughly enjoyable book; Quidditch fans are sure to find it both instructive and entertaining.'

Editor, *Which Broomstick?*

Brutus Scrimgeour

'The definitive work on the origins and history of Quidditch. Highly recommended.'

Brutus Scrimgeour, author, *The Beaters' Bible*

★ *'Mr Whisp shows a lot of promise.*
If he keeps up the good work, he may well
find himself sharing a photoshoot
with me one of these days!'
Gilderoy Lockhart, author, *Magical Me*

★ *'Bet you anything it'll be a bestseller.*
Go on, I bet you.'
Ludovic Bagman, England and Wimbourne Wasps Beater

★ *'I've read worse.'*
Rita Skeeter, *Daily Prophet*

THE HARRY POTTER SERIES

In reading order:
Harry Potter and the Philosopher's Stone
Harry Potter and the Chamber of Secrets
Harry Potter and the Prisoner of Azkaban
Harry Potter and the Goblet of Fire
Harry Potter and the Order of the Phoenix
Harry Potter and the Half-Blood Prince
Harry Potter and the Deathly Hallows

Also available in Latin:
Harry Potter and the Philosopher's Stone
Harry Potter and the Chamber of Secrets

Also available in Welsh, Ancient Greek and Irish:
Harry Potter and the Philosopher's Stone

COMPANION VOLUMES

Fantastic Beasts and Where to Find Them
Quidditch Through the Ages
(Published in aid of Comic Relief and Lumos)

The Tales of Beedle the Bard
(Published in aid of Lumos)

The three companion volumes also available as:
The Hogwarts Library
(Published in aid of Comic Relief and Lumos)

ILLUSTRATED EDITIONS

Illustrated by Jim Kay
Harry Potter and the Philosopher's Stone
Harry Potter and the Chamber of Secrets
Harry Potter and the Prisoner of Azkaban
Harry Potter and the Goblet of Fire

Illustrated by Olivia Lomenech Gill
Fantastic Beasts and Where to Find Them

Illustrated by Chris Riddell
The Tales of Beedle the Bard

J.K. ROWLING
QUIDDITCH THROUGH THE AGES

KENNILWORTHY WHISP

ILLUSTRATED BY
EMILY GRAVETT

BLOOMSBURY
CHILDREN'S BOOKS
LONDON OXFORD NEW YORK NEW DELHI SYDNEY

in association with

Whizz Hard
Books
129B DIAGON ALLEY, LONDON

For Oleander
E.G.

BLOOMSBURY CHILDREN'S BOOKS
Bloomsbury Publishing Plc
50 Bedford Square, London, WC1B 3DP, UK

BLOOMSBURY, BLOOMSBURY CHILDREN'S BOOKS and the Diana logo
are trademarks of Bloomsbury Publishing Plc

First published in Great Britain in 2001 by Bloomsbury Publishing Plc
This edition published in 2020

A catalogue record for this book is available from the British Library

ISBN 978 1 5266 0812 3
1 3 5 7 9 10 8 6 4 2

Printed and bound in China

Comic Relief (UK) was set up in 1985 by a group of British comedians to raise funds for projects promoting
social justice and helping to tackle poverty. Monies from the worldwide sales of this book will go to help
children and young people in the UK and around the world, preparing them to be ready for the future –
to be safe, healthy, educated and empowered. Comic Relief is the trading name of Charity Projects,
a registered charity in the UK with charity nos. 326568 (England/Wales) and SC039730 (Scotland).

Named after the light-giving spell in the Harry Potter books, Lumos was set up by
J.K. Rowling to end the use of orphanages and institutions for vulnerable children around the
world by 2050 and ensure all future generations of children can be raised in loving families.
Lumos is the operating name of Lumos Foundation, a company limited by guarantee
registered in England and Wales, number 5611912. Registered charity number 1112575.

All papers used by Bloomsbury Publishing Plc are natural, recyclable products from
wood grown in well managed forests. The manufacturing processes conform
to the environmental regulations of the country of origin

ACKNOWLEDGEMENTS
p.xv photograph used by courtesy of Terry Gravett; p.62 photograph of Jubilee Rock,
Blisland, Bodmin Moor from the George Ellis Collection (reference no. C.171) used by
kind permission of the Archives and Cornish Studies Service, Kresen Kernow, Redruth.

With thanks to J.K. Rowling for creating this book and so generously giving all her royalties from it to Comic Relief and Lumos

CONTENTS

Professor Albus Dumbledore, with Fawkes, his beloved pet phoenix

FOREWORD

QUIDDITCH THROUGH THE AGES is one of the most popular titles in the Hogwarts school library. Madam Pince, our librarian, tells me that it is 'pawed about, dribbled on and generally maltreated' nearly every day – a high compliment for any book. Anyone who plays or watches Quidditch regularly will relish Mr Whisp's book, as do those of us interested in wider wizarding history. As we have developed the game of Quidditch, so it has developed us; Quidditch unites witches and wizards from all walks of life, bringing us together to share moments of exhilaration, triumph and (for those who support the Chudley Cannons) despair.

It was with some difficulty, I must own, that I persuaded Madam Pince to part with one of her books so that it might be copied for wider consumption. Indeed, when I told her it was to be made available to Muggles, she was rendered temporarily speechless and neither moved nor blinked for several minutes. When she came to herself she was thoughtful enough to ask whether I had taken leave of my senses. I was pleased to reassure her on that point and went on to explain why I had taken this unprecedented decision.

Muggle readers will need no introduction to the work of Comic Relief and Lumos, so I now repeat my explanation to Madam Pince for the benefit of witches and wizards who have purchased this book. Comic Relief harnesses laughter to fight poverty and injustice in a most imaginative way, using it to raise funds to help save and improve lives – a brand of magic to which we all aspire. Lumos, in turn, brings light to the darkest of places, revealing children hidden from the world and guiding them home. By buying this book – and I would advise you to buy it, because if you read it for too long without handing over money you will find yourself the object of a Thief's Curse – you too will be contributing to this magical mission.

I would be deceiving my readers if I said that this explanation made Madam Pince happy about handing over a library book to Muggles. She suggested several alternatives, such as telling the people from Comic Relief and Lumos that the library had burned down, or simply pretending that I had dropped dead without leaving instructions. When I told her that on the whole I preferred my original plan, she reluctantly agreed to hand over the book, though at the point when it came to let go of it, her nerve failed her and I was forced to prise her fingers individually from the spine.

Although I have removed the usual library-book spells from this volume, I cannot promise that every trace has gone. Madam Pince has been known to add unusual jinxes to the books in her care. I myself doodled absent-mindedly on a copy of *Theories of Transubstantial Transfiguration* last year and next moment found the book beating me fiercely around the head. Please be careful how you treat this book. Do not rip out the pages. Do not drop it in the bath. I cannot promise that Madam Pince will not swoop down on you, wherever you are, and demand a heavy fine.

All that remains is for me to thank you for supporting Comic Relief and Lumos and to beg Muggles not to try Quidditch at home; it is, of course, an entirely fictional sport and nobody really plays it. May I also take this opportunity to wish Puddlemere United the best of luck next season.

Popular titles by
Kennilworthy Whisp

ABOUT THE AUTHOR

KENNILWORTHY WHISP IS A renowned Quidditch expert (and, he says, fanatic). He is the author of many Quidditch-related works, including *The Wonder of Wigtown Wanderers*, *He Flew Like a Madman* (a biography of 'Dangerous Dai' Llewellyn) and *Beating the Bludgers – A Study of Defensive Strategies in Quidditch*. Kennilworthy Whisp divides his time between his home in Nottinghamshire and 'wherever Wigtown Wanderers are playing this week'. His hobbies include backgammon, vegetarian cookery and collecting vintage broomsticks.

CHAPTER ONE

The Evolution of the
Flying Broomstick

N O SPELL YET DEVISED enables wizards to fly unaided in human form. Those few Animagi who transform into winged creatures may enjoy flight, but they are a rarity. The witch or wizard who finds him- or herself Transfigured into a bat may take to the air, but, having a bat's brain, they are sure to forget where they want to go the moment they take flight. Levitation is commonplace, but our ancestors were not content with hovering five feet from the ground. They wanted more. They wanted to fly like birds, but without the inconvenience of growing feathers.

 Unknown witch or warlock's notebook depicting early attempts to find a spell for human flight

We are so accustomed these days to the fact that every wizarding household in Britain owns at least one flying broomstick that we rarely stop to ask ourselves why. Why should the humble broom have become the one object legally allowed as a means of wizarding transport? Why did we in the West not adopt the carpet so beloved of our Eastern brethren? Why didn't we choose to produce flying barrels, flying armchairs, flying bathtubs – why brooms?

Medieval Ash Broom

Shrewd enough to see that their Muggle neighbours would seek to exploit their powers if they knew their full extent, witches and wizards kept themselves to themselves long before the International Statute of Wizarding Secrecy came into effect. If they were to keep a means of flight in their houses, it would necessarily be something discreet, something easy to hide. The broomstick was ideal for this purpose; it required no explanation, no excuse if found by Muggles, it was easily portable and inexpensive. Nevertheless, the first brooms bewitched for flying purposes had their drawbacks.

Fig. A Medieval broomstick on display in the Museum of Quidditch, London

Records show that witches and wizards in Europe were using flying broomsticks as early as AD 962. A German illuminated manuscript of this period shows three warlocks dismounting from their brooms with looks of exquisite discomfort on their faces. Guthrie Lochrin, a Scottish wizard writing in 1107, spoke of the 'splinter-filled buttocks and bulging piles' he suffered after a short broom ride from Montrose to Arbroath.

A medieval broomstick on display in the Museum of Quidditch in London gives us an insight into Lochrin's discomfort (see Fig. A on pages 4–5). A thick knotty handle of unvarnished ash, with hazel twigs bound crudely to one end, it is neither comfortable nor aerodynamic. The charms placed upon it are similarly basic: it will only move forwards at one speed; it will go up, down and stop.

German illuminated manuscript on vellum, showing three warlocks dismounting from their brooms (late 10th century)

As wizarding families in those days made their own brooms, there was enormous variation in the speed, comfort and handling of the transport available to them. By the twelfth century, however, wizards had learned to barter services, so that a skilled maker of brooms could exchange them for the potions his neighbour might make better than himself. Once broomsticks became more comfortable, they were flown for pleasure rather than merely used as a means of getting from point A to point B.

CHAPTER TWO

Ancient Broom
Games

BROOM SPORTS EMERGED almost as soon as broomsticks were sufficiently advanced to allow fliers to turn corners and vary their speed and height. Early wizarding writings and paintings give us some idea of the games our ancestors played. Some of these no longer exist; others have survived or evolved into the sports we know today.

The celebrated **ANNUAL BROOM RACE** of Sweden dates from the tenth century. Fliers race from Kopparberg to Arjeplog, a distance of slightly over three hundred miles. The course runs straight through a dragon reservation and the vast silver trophy is shaped like a Swedish Short-Snout. Nowadays this is an international event and wizards of all nationalities congregate at Kopparberg to cheer the starters, then Apparate to Arjeplog to congratulate the survivors.

Poster for the 1956 race from Kopparberg to Arjeplog, a distance of forty-eight Swedish miles

Woodcut map of the route (medieval)

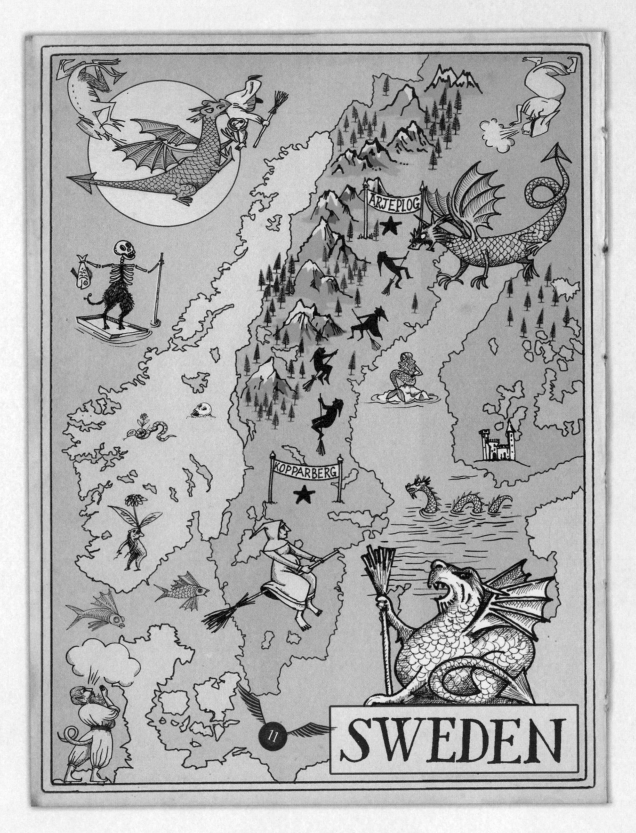

'The course runs straight
through a dragon reservation.'

The famous painting *Günther der Gewalttätige ist der Gewinner* ('Gunther the Violent is the Winner'), dated 1105, shows the ancient German game of **STICHSTOCK**. A twenty-foot-high pole was topped with an inflated dragon bladder. One player on a broomstick had the job of protecting this bladder. The bladder-guardian was tied to the pole by a rope around his or her waist, so that he or she could not fly further than ten feet away from it. The rest of the players would take it in turns to fly at the bladder and attempt to puncture it with the specially sharpened ends of their brooms. The bladder-guardian was allowed to use his or her wand to repel these attacks. The game ended when the bladder was successfully punctured, or the bladder-guardian had either succeeded in hexing all opponents out of the running or collapsed from exhaustion. Stichstock died out in the fourteenth century.

13

Günther der Gewalttätige ist der Gewinner ('Gunther the Violent is the Winner'), tempera painting on wood panel (1105)

Cover of one of the many examples of sheet music produced on the subject of Fingal the Fearless (19th century)

'The legendary wizard Fingal the Fearless is alleged to have been an Aingingein champion.'

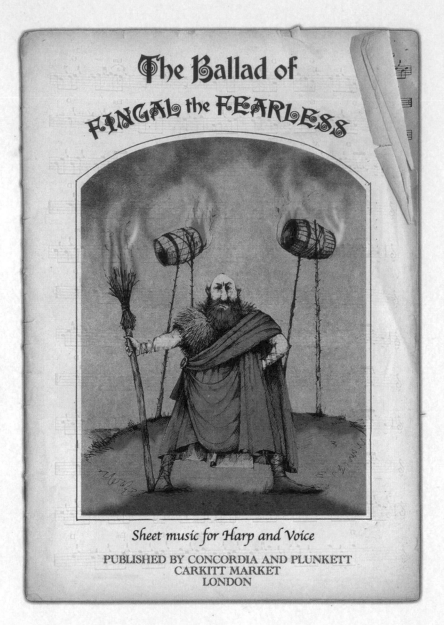

The Ballad of FINGAL the FEARLESS

Sheet music for Harp and Voice

PUBLISHED BY CONCORDIA AND PLUNKETT
CARKITT MARKET
LONDON

In Ireland the game of **AINGINGEIN** flourished, the subject of many an Irish ballad (the legendary wizard Fingal the Fearless is alleged to have been an Aingingein champion). One by one the players would take the Dom, or ball (actually the gall bladder of a goat), and speed through a series of burning barrels set high in the air on stilts. The Dom was to be thrown through the final barrel. The player who succeeded in getting the Dom

14

through the last barrel in the fastest time, without having caught fire on the way, was the winner.

Scotland was the birthplace of what is probably the most dangerous of all broom games – CREAOTHCEANN. The game features in a tragic Gaelic poem of the eleventh century, the first verse of which says, in translation:

The players assembled, twelve fine, hearty men,
They strapped on their cauldrons, stood poised to fly,
At the sound of the horn they were swiftly airborne
But ten of their number were fated to die.

Creaothceann players each wore a cauldron strapped to the head. At the sound of the horn or drum, up to a hundred charmed rocks and boulders that had been hovering a hundred feet above the ground began to fall towards the earth. The Creaothceann players zoomed around trying to catch as many rocks as possible in their cauldrons. Considered by many Scottish wizards to be the supreme test of manliness and courage, Creaothceann enjoyed considerable popularity in the Middle Ages, despite the huge number of fatalities that resulted from it. The game was made illegal in 1762, and though Magnus 'Dent-Head' Macdonald spearheaded a campaign for its reintroduction in the 1960s, the Ministry of Magic refused to lift the ban.

Shuntbumps was popular in Devon, England. This was a crude form of jousting, the sole aim being to knock as many other players as possible off their brooms, the last person remaining on their broom winning.

CHAP 4. SPORTS AND PASTIMES OF THE WIZARDING WORLD 428

Shuntbumps. A common game in Devon

Illustration depicting a game of Shuntbumps, from *Sports and Pastimes of the Wizarding World* (19th century)

SWIVENHODGE began in Herefordshire. Like Stichstock, this involved an inflated bladder, usually a pig's. Players sat backwards on their brooms and batted the bladder backwards and forwards across a hedge with the brush ends of their brooms. The first person to miss gave their opponent a point. First to reach fifty points was the winner.

'Players sat backwards on their brooms and batted the bladder backwards and forwards across a hedge with the brush ends of their brooms.'

Swivenhodge is still played in England, though it has never achieved much widespread popularity; Shuntbumps survives only as a children's game. At Queerditch Marsh, however, a game had been created that would one day become the most popular in the wizarding world.

CHAPTER THREE

The Game from
Queerditch Marsh

WE OWE OUR KNOWLEDGE of the rude beginnings of Quidditch to the writings of the witch Gertie Keddle, who lived on the edge of Queerditch Marsh in the eleventh century. Fortunately for us, she kept a diary, now in the Museum of Quidditch in London.

 Gertie Keddle's Anglo-Saxon diary, with an illustration of the back-to-front knee curse, held in the Museum of Quidditch, London (11th century)

The excerpts below have been translated from the badly spelled Saxon of the original.

Tuesday. Hot. That lot from across the marsh haue been at it again. Playing a stupid game on their broomsticks. A big leather ball landed in my cabbages. I hexed the man who came for it. I'd like to see him fly with his knees on back to front, the great hairy hog.

Tuesday. Wet. Was out on the marsh picking nettles. Broomstick idiots playing again. Watched for a bit from behind a rock. They'ue got a new ball. Throwing it to each other and trying to stick it in trees at either end of the marsh. Pointless rubbish.

Tuesday. Windy. Gwenog came for nettle tea, then inuited me out for a treat. Ended up watching those numbskulls playing their game on the marsh. That big Scottish warlock from up the hill was there. Now they'ue got two big heauy rocks flying around trying to knock them all off their brooms. Vnfortunately didn't happen while I was watching. Gwenog told me she often played herself. Went home in disgust.

These extracts reveal much more than Gertie Keddle could have guessed, quite apart from the fact that she only knew the name of one of the days of the week. Firstly, the ball that landed in her cabbage patch was made of leather, as is the modern Quaffle – naturally, the inflated bladder used in other broom games of the period would be difficult to throw accurately, particularly in windy conditions.

'Now they've got two big heavy rocks flying around trying to knock them all off their brooms.'
Gertie Keddle

Secondly, Gertie tells us that the men were 'trying to stick it in trees at either end of the marsh' – apparently an early form of goalscoring. Thirdly, she gives us a glimpse of the forerunners of Bludgers. It is immensely interesting that there was a 'big Scottish warlock' present. Could he have been a Creaothceann player? Was it his idea to bewitch heavy rocks to zoom dangerously around the pitch, inspired by the boulders used in his native game?

We find no further mention of the sport played on Queerditch Marsh until a century later, when the wizard Goodwin Kneen took up his quill to write to his Norwegian cousin Olaf. Kneen lived in Yorkshire, which demonstrates the spread of the sport throughout Britain in the hundred years after Gertie Keddle first witnessed it. Kneen's letter is deposited in the archives of the Norwegian Ministry of Magic.

Goodwin Kneen's bronze seal
(12th century)

Dear Olaf

How are you? I am well though Gunnhilda has got a touch of dragon pox. We enjoyed a spirited game of Kwidditch last Saturday night, though poor Gunnhilda was not up to playing Catcher, and we had to use Radulf the Blacksmith instead. The team from Ilkley played well though was no match for us, for we had been practising hard all month and scored forty-two times. Radulf got a Blooder in the head because old Ugga wasn't quick enough with his club. The new scoring

Original letter sent by Goodwin Kneen to his cousin Olaf, held in the archives of the Norwegian Ministry of Magic (12th century)

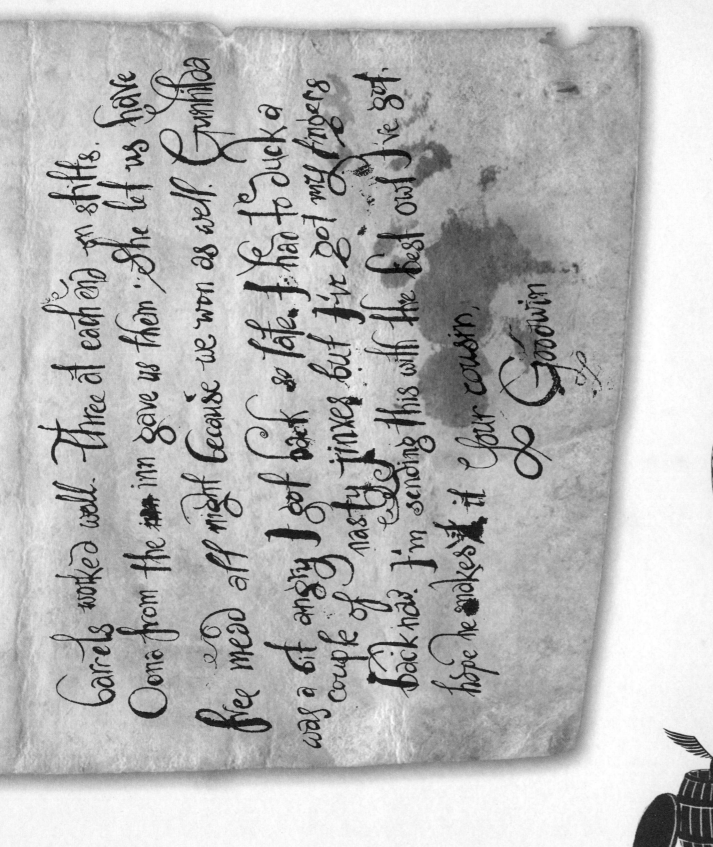

barrels worked well. Three at each end on stilts. Oona from the inn gave us them. "She let us have free mead all night because we won as well. Gunhilda was a bit angry I got back so late. I had to duck a couple of nasty jinxes but I've got my fingers back now. I'm sending this with the best owl I've got. hope he makes it to your cousin,

Goodwin

Here we see how far the game has progressed in a century. Goodwin's wife was to have played 'Catcher' – probably the old term for Chaser. The 'Blooder' (undoubtedly Bludger) that hit Radulf the blacksmith should have been fended off by Ugga, who was obviously playing Beater, as he was carrying a club. The goals are no longer trees, but barrels on stilts. One crucial element in the game was still missing, however: the Golden Snitch. The addition of the fourth Quidditch ball did not occur until the middle of the thirteenth century and it came about in a curious manner.

CHAPTER FOUR

The Arrival of the
Golden Snitch

PROFICISCVNTVR : HIC

Tapestry depicting a medieval Snidget hunt, displayed in the Museum of Quidditch, London (12th century)

FROM THE EARLY 1100S, Snidget-hunting had been popular among many witches and wizards. The Golden Snidget (see Fig. B opposite) is today a protected species, but at that time Golden Snidgets were common in northern Europe, though difficult to detect by Muggles because of their aptitude at hiding and their very great speed.

The diminutive size of the Snidget, coupled with its remarkable agility in the air and talent at avoiding predators, merely added to the prestige of wizards who caught them. A twelfth-century tapestry preserved in the Museum of Quidditch shows a group setting out to catch a Snidget. In the first portion of the tapestry, some hunters carry nets, others use wands, and still others attempt to catch the Snidget with their bare hands. The tapestry reveals the fact that the Snidget was often crushed by its captor. In the final portion of the tapestry we see the wizard who caught the Snidget being presented with a bag of gold.

Snidget-hunting was reprehensible in many ways. Every right-minded wizard must deplore the destruction of these peace-loving little birds in the name of sport. Moreover, Snidget-hunting, which was usually undertaken in broad daylight, led to more Muggle broomstick sightings than any other pursuit. The Wizards' Council of the time, however, was unable to curb the sport's popularity – indeed, it appears that the Council itself saw little wrong with it, as we shall see.

Snidget-hunting finally crossed paths with Quidditch in 1269 at a game attended by the Chief of the Wizards' Council himself, Barberus Bragge. We know this because of the eyewitness account sent by Madam Modesty Rabnott of Kent to her sister

Fig. B Golden Snidgets were common in northern Europe, though difficult to detect by Muggles because of their aptitude for hiding and their very great speed.

HIC · VENATOR · AVRVM · ACCIPIT

AVIS · INTERFECTA · EST:

Prudence in Aberdeen (this letter is also on display in the Museum of Quidditch). According to Madam Rabnott, Bragge brought a caged Snidget to the match and told the assembled players that he would award one hundred and fifty Galleons[1] to the player who caught it during the course of the game. Madam Rabnott explains what happened next:

Letter from Modesty Rabnott to her sister, Prudence (1269)

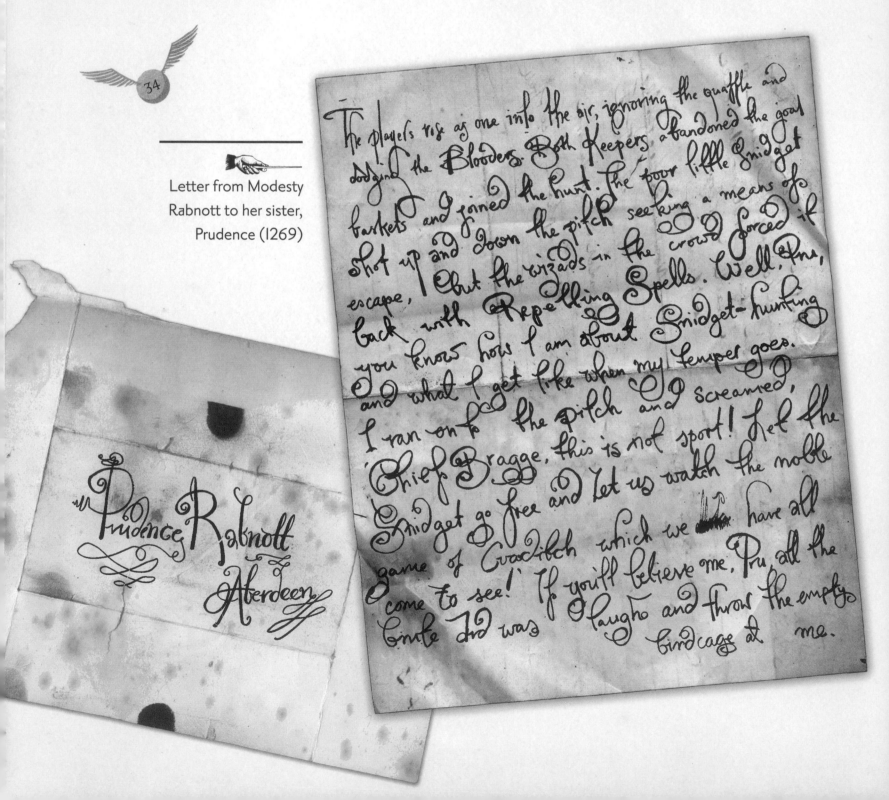

The players rise as one into the air, ignoring the quaffle and dodging the Bludgers. Both Keepers abandoned the goal baskets and joined the hunt. The four little Snidget shot up and down the pitch seeking a means of escape, but the wizards in the crowd forced it back with Repelling Spells. Well, Pru, you know how I am about Snidget-hunting and what I get like when my temper goes. I ran onto the pitch and I screamed, 'Chief Bragge, this is not sport! Let the Snidget go free and let us watch the noble game of Quidditch which we have all come to see!' If you'll believe me, Pru, all the brute did was laugh and throw the empty birdcage at me.

Prudence Rabnott
Aberdeen

Well, I saw red, Pru, I really did. When the poor little Snidget flew my way I did a Summoning Charm. You know how good my Summoning Charms are, Pru – of course it was easier for me to aim properly, not being mounted on a broomstick at the time. The little bird came zooming into my hand. I stuffed it down the front of my robes and ran like fury.

Well, they caught me, but not before I'd got out of the crowds and released the Snidget. Chief Bragge was very angry and for a moment I thought I'd end up a horned toad, or worse, but luckily his advisers calmed him down and I was only fined ten Galleons for disrupting the game. Of course I've never had ten Galleons in my life, so that's the old home gone.

I'll be coming to live with you shortly. Luckily they didn't take the Hippogriff. And I'll tell you this, Pru, Chief Bragge would have lost my vote if I'd had one.

Your loving sister
Modesty
x x

Madam Rabnott's brave action might have saved one Snidget, but she could not save them all. Chief Bragge's idea had for ever changed the nature of Quidditch. Golden Snidgets were soon being released during

---

1. Equivalent to over a million Galleons today. Whether Chief Bragge intended to pay or not is a moot point.

all Quidditch games, one player on each team (the Hunter) having the sole task of catching it. When the bird was killed, the game was over and the Hunter's team was awarded an extra one hundred and fifty points, in memory of the one hundred and fifty Galleons promised by Chief Bragge. The crowd undertook to keep the Snidget on the pitch by using the Repelling Spells mentioned by Madam Rabnott.

By the middle of the following century, however, Golden Snidget numbers had fallen so low that the Wizards' Council, now headed by the considerably more enlightened Elfrida Clagg, made the Golden Snidget a protected species, outlawing both its killing and its use in Quidditch games. The Modesty Rabnott Snidget Reservation was founded in Somerset and a substitute for the bird was frantically sought to enable the game of Quidditch to proceed.

The invention of the Golden Snitch is credited to the wizard Bowman Wright of Godric's Hollow. While Quidditch teams all over the country tried to find bird substitutes for the Snidget, Wright, who was a skilled metal-charmer, set himself to the task of creating a ball that mimicked the behaviour and flight patterns of the Snidget. That he succeeded perfectly is clear from the many rolls of parchment he left behind him on his death (now in the possession of a private collector), listing the orders

Bowman Wright's manuscript showing early Snitch designs (14th century)

that he had received from all over the country. The Golden Snitch, as Bowman called his invention, was a walnut-sized ball exactly the weight of a Snidget. Its silvery wings had rotational joints like the Snidget's, enabling it to change direction with the lightning speed and precision of its living model. Unlike the Snidget, however, the Snitch had been bewitched to remain within the boundaries of the field. The introduction of the Golden Snitch may be said to have finished the process begun three hundred years before on Queerditch Marsh. Quidditch had been truly born.

CHAPTER FIVE

Anti-Muggle
Precautions

IN 1398 THE WIZARD Zacharias Mumps set down the first full description of the game of Quidditch. He began by emphasising the need for anti-Muggle security while playing the game:

Choose areas of deserted moorland far from Muggle habitations and make sure that you cannot be seen once you take off on your brooms. Muggle-repelling charms are useful if you are setting up a permanent pitch. It is advisable, too, to play at night.

We deduce that Mumps's excellent advice was not always followed from the fact that the Wizards' Council outlawed all Quidditch-playing within fifty miles of towns in 1362. Clearly the popularity of the game was increasing rapidly, for the

Muggle-repelling charm on parchment, origin unknown (medieval)

Portrait of Zacharias Mumps, oil painting on wood panel (15th century)

'It is advisable, too, to play at night.'
Zacharias Mumps

Council found it necessary to amend the ban in 1368, making it illegal to play within a hundred miles of a town. In 1419, the Council issued the famously worded decree that Quidditch should not be played 'anywhere near any place where there is the slightest chance that a Muggle might be watching or we'll see how well you can play whilst chained to a dungeon wall'.

As every school-age wizard knows, the fact that we fly on broomsticks is probably our worst-kept secret. No Muggle illustration of a witch is complete without a broom and however ludicrous these drawings are (for none of the broomsticks depicted by Muggles could stay up in the air for a moment), they remind us that we were careless for too many centuries to be surprised that broomsticks and magic are inextricably linked in the Muggle mind.

Adequate security measures were not enforced until the International Statute of Wizarding Secrecy of 1692 made every Ministry of Magic directly responsible for the consequences of magical sports played within their territories. This subsequently led, in Britain, to the formation of

Here is a witch.
The witch is flying
on a broomstick.

 A typical Muggle illustration of a witch
flying on a broomstick (20th century)

the Department of Magical Games and Sports. Quidditch teams that flouted the Ministry guidelines were henceforth forced to disband. The most famous instance of this was the Banchory Bangers, a Scottish team renowned not only for their poor Quidditch skills but also for their post-match parties. After their 1814 match against the Appleby Arrows (see Chapter Seven), the Bangers not only allowed their Bludgers to zoom away into the night, but also set out to capture a Hebridean Black for their team mascot. Ministry of Magic representatives apprehended them as they were flying over Inverness and the Banchory Bangers never played again.

Nowadays Quidditch teams do not play locally, but travel to pitches which have been set up by the Department of Magical Games and Sports where adequate anti-Muggle security is maintained. As Zacharias Mumps so rightly suggested six hundred years ago, Quidditch pitches are safest on deserted moors.

CHAPTER SIX

Changes in Quidditch Since the Fourteenth Century

PITCH

ZACHARIAS MUMPS DESCRIBES the fourteenth-century pitch as oval-shaped, five hundred feet long and a hundred and eighty feet wide with a small central circle (approximately two feet in diameter) in the middle. Mumps tells us that the referee (or Quijudge, as he or she was then known) carried the four balls into this central circle while the fourteen players stood around him. The moment the balls were released (the Quaffle was

 Fig. C Goalposts circa 1398 were large baskets.

 Miniature portrait of Quintius Umfraville (17th century)

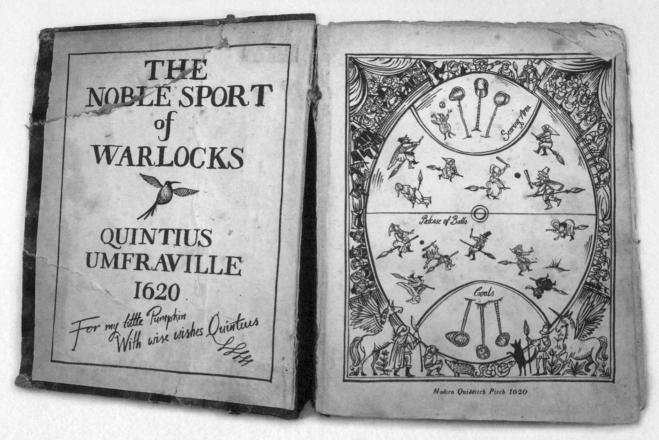

THE
NOBLE SPORT
of
WARLOCKS

QUINTIUS
UMFRAVILLE
1620

For my little Pumpkin With wise wishes Quintius

Modern Quidditch Pitch 1620

 Fig. D Diagram of the seventeenth-century pitch, from *The Noble Sport of Warlocks* (1620)

thrown by the referee; see 'The Quaffle' below), the players raced into the air. The goalposts in Mumps's time were still large baskets on poles, as seen in Fig. C.

In 1620 Quintius Umfraville wrote a book called *The Noble Sport of Warlocks*, which included a diagram of the seventeenth-century pitch (see Fig. D).

Early manuscript illumination depicting the Quijudge carrying
the four balls into the centre during a game (14th century)

No. 12, 946   Monday 12th February 1883

"BRING BACK OUR BASKETS!"

That was the cry heard from Quidditch players across the nation last night as it became clear that the Department of Magical Games and Sports had decided to burn the baskets used for centuries for goalscoring in Quidditch.

'We're not burning them, don't exaggerate,' said an irritable-looking departmental representative last night when asked to comment. 'Baskets, as you may have noticed, come in different sizes. We have found it impossible to standardise basket size so as to make goalposts throughout Britain equal. Surely you can see it's a matter of fairness. I mean, there's a team up near Barnton, they've got these minuscule little baskets attached to the opposing team's posts, you couldn't get a grape in them. And up their own end they've got these great wicker caves swinging around. It's not on. We've settled on a fixed hoop size and that's it. Everything nice and fair.'

At this point, the departmental

representative was forced to retreat under a hail of baskets thrown by the angry demonstrators assembled in the hall. Although the ensuing riot was later blamed on goblin agitators, there can be no doubt that Quidditch fans across Britain are tonight mourning the

end of the game as we know it.

''T won't be t' same wi'out baskets,' said one apple-cheeked old wizard sadly. 'I remember when I were a lad, we used to set fire to 'em for a laugh during t' match. You can't do that with goal hoops. 'Alf t' fun's gone.'

Quaffle pre-1711

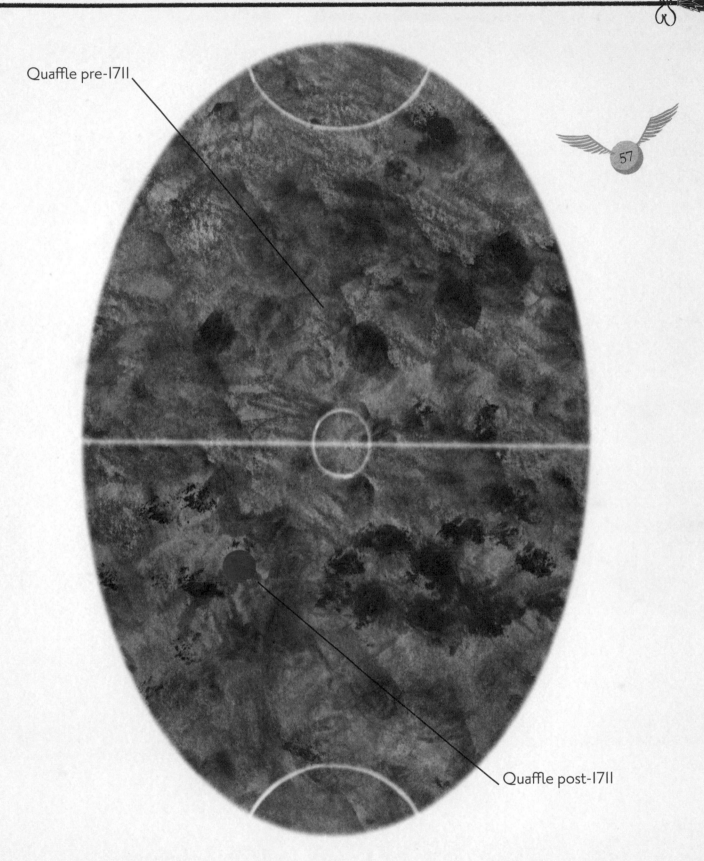

57

Quaffle post-1711

'The modern quaffle was first coloured scarlet in the winter of 1711,
after a game when heavy rain had made it indistinguishable
from the muddy ground whenever it was dropped.'

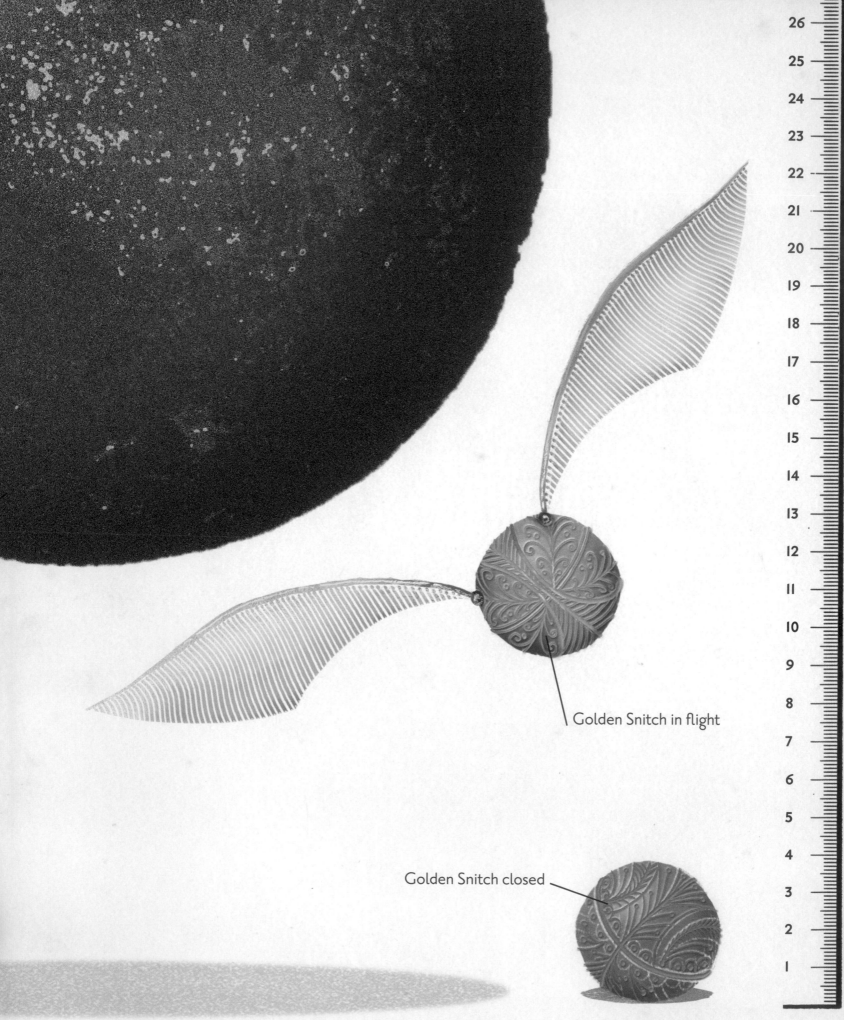

Golden Snitch in flight

Golden Snitch closed

QUIDDITCH BALLS
ACTUAL SIZE

INCHES
10
9
8
7
6
5
4
3
2
1

BALLS

THE QUAFFLE

As we know from Gertie Keddle's diary, the Quaffle was from earliest times made of leather. Alone of the four Quidditch balls, the Quaffle was not originally enchanted, but merely a patched leather ball, often with a strap (see Fig. E below), as it had to be caught and thrown one-handed.

ANCIENT QUAFFLES

MODERN QUAFFLES

Pre-Pennifold
Quaffle

Pennifold
Quaffle

 Fig. E The development of the Quaffle

Copy of the *Daily Prophet*, 12th February 1883

Here we see the addition of what we know as 'scoring areas' (see 'Rules' below). The baskets on top of the goalposts were considerably smaller and higher than in Mumps's time.

By 1883 baskets had ceased to be used for scoring and were replaced with the goalposts we use today, an innovation reported in the *Daily Prophet* of the time (see opposite). The Quidditch pitch has not altered since that time.

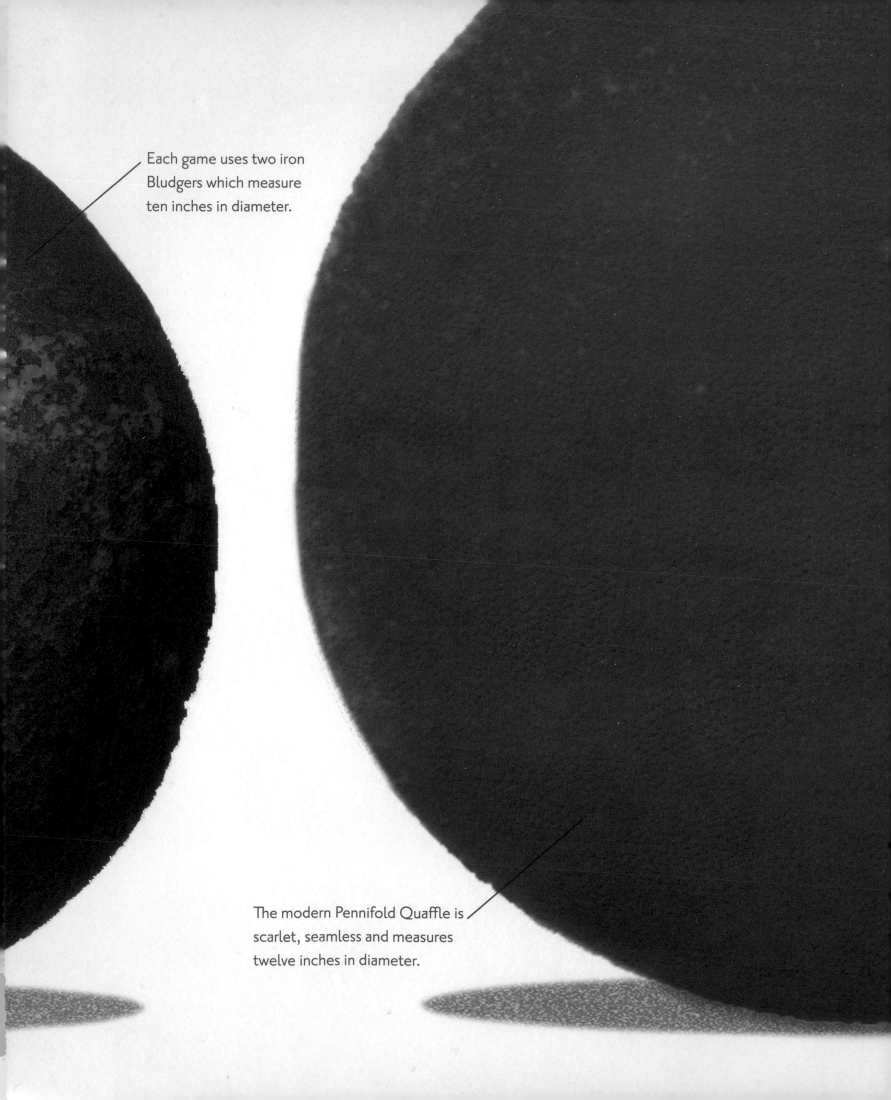

Each game uses two iron Bludgers which measure ten inches in diameter.

The modern Pennifold Quaffle is scarlet, seamless and measures twelve inches in diameter.

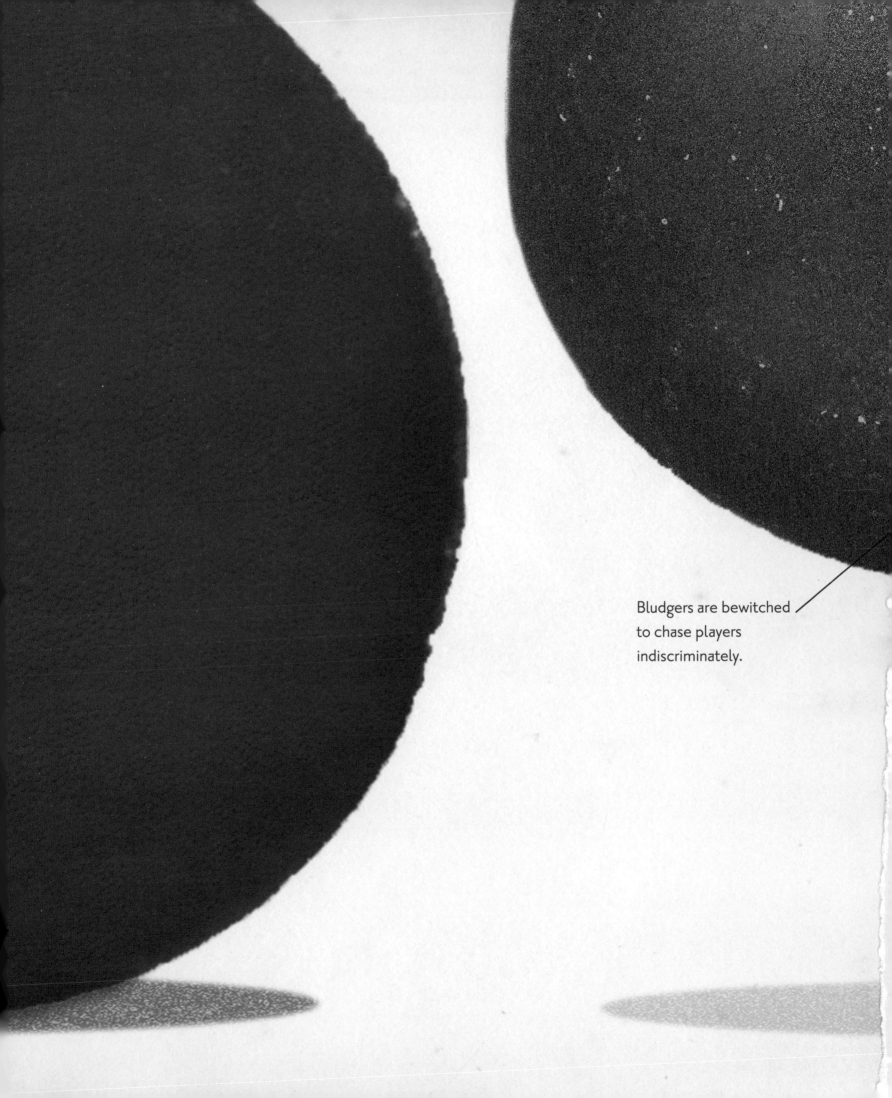

Bludgers are bewitched
to chase players
indiscriminately.

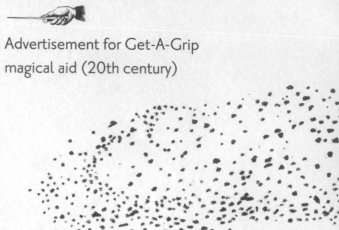

Advertisement for Get-A-Grip
magical aid (20th century)

Some old Quaffles have finger holes. With the discovery of Gripping Charms in 1875, however, straps and finger holes have become unnecessary, as the Chaser is able to keep a one-handed hold on the charmed leather without such aids.

The modern Quaffle is twelve inches in diameter and seamless. It was first coloured scarlet in the winter of 1711, after a game when heavy rain had made it indistinguishable from the muddy ground whenever it was dropped. Chasers were also becoming increasingly irritated by the necessity of diving continually towards the ground to retrieve the Quaffle whenever they missed a catch and so, shortly after the Quaffle's change of colour, the witch Daisy Pennifold had the idea of bewitching the Quaffle so that if dropped, it would fall slowly earthwards as though sinking through water, meaning that Chasers could grab it in mid-air. The Pennifold Quaffle is still used today.

*'Players would be pursued
by flying gravel.'*

THE BLUDGERS

The first Bludgers (or 'Blooders') were, as we have seen, flying rocks, and in Mumps's time they had merely progressed to rocks carved into the shape of balls. These had one important disadvantage, however: they could be cracked by the magically reinforced Beaters' bats of the fifteenth century, in which case all players would be pursued by flying gravel for the remainder of the game.

It was probably for this reason that some Quidditch teams began experimenting with metal Bludgers in the early sixteenth century.

 Illustration of an early
Bludger (or just a rock)

 By the fourteenth century the rock
Bludgers were being shaped into balls.

Agatha Chubb, expert in ancient wizarding artefacts, has identified no fewer than twelve lead Bludgers dating from this period, discovered both in Irish peat bogs and English marshes. 'They are undoubtedly Bludgers rather than cannonballs,' she writes.

The faint indentations of magically reinforced Beater's bats are visible and one can see the distinctive hallmarks of manufacture by a wizard (as opposed to a Muggle) – the smoothness of line, the perfect symmetry. A final clue was the fact that each and every one of them whizzed around my study and attempted to knock me to the floor when released from its case.

Agatha Chubb

— me being chased

Notebook belonging to Agatha Chubb and photograph taken during an artefact dig (1913)

Lead was eventually discovered to be too soft for the purpose of Bludger manufacture (any indentation left on a Bludger will affect its ability to fly straight). Nowadays all Bludgers are made of iron. They are ten inches in diameter.

Bludgers are bewitched to chase players indiscriminately. If left to their own devices, they will attack the player closest to them, hence the Beaters' task is to knock the Bludgers as far away from their own team as possible.

Crymlyn Bog
(Wales)
circa 1507

Queerditch Marsh
(England)
circa 1511

Ballynahone Bog
(Ireland)
circa 1533

Cors Caron
(Wales)
circa 1512

Bog of Allen
(Ireland)
circa 1520

Flow Country
(Scotland)
circa 1526

Moine Mhor
(Scotland)
circa 1522

Yanal Bog
(England)
circa 1500

Boora Bog
(Ireland)
circa 1510

Doxey Marshes
(England)
circa 1510

Romney Marsh
(England)
circa 1509

Minsmere Marsh
(England)
circa 1539

Agatha Chubb's stunning collection of Bludgers found by her in various marshes and bogs of Ireland and the United Kingdom

THE GOLDEN SNITCH

The Golden Snitch is walnut-sized, as was the Golden Snidget. It is bewitched to evade capture for as long as possible. There is a tale that a Golden Snitch evaded capture for six months on Bodmin Moor in 1884, both teams finally giving up in disgust at their Seekers' poor performances. Cornish wizards familiar with the area insist to this day that the Snitch is still living wild on the moor, though I have not been able to confirm this story.

ACTUAL SIZE

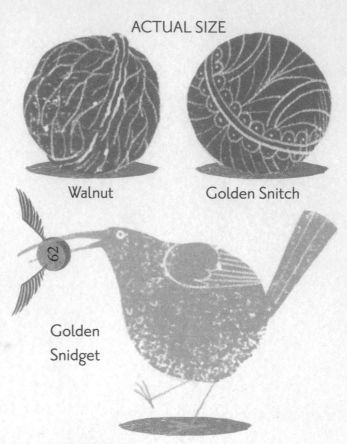

Walnut   Golden Snitch

Golden
Snidget

C. 171

 Postcard of Bodmin Moor, where the famous 'Golden Snitch of 1884' is said to have been sighted

PLAYERS

THE KEEPER

The position of Keeper has certainly existed since the thirteenth century (see Chapter Four), though the role has changed since that time. According to Zacharias Mumps:

The Keeper should be first to reach the goal baskets for it is his job to prevent the Quaffle entering therein. The Keeper should beware of straying too far towards the other end of the pitch, in case his baskets come under threat in his absence. However, a fast Keeper may be able to score a goal and then return to his baskets in time to prevent the other team equalising. It is a matter for the individual conscience of the Keeper.

Page from an early printed edition of Zacharius Mumps's writings, with an illustration of a Keeper (15th century)

It is clear from this that in Mumps's day the Keepers performed like Chasers with extra responsibilities. They were allowed to move all over the pitch and to score goals.

By the time Quintius Umfraville wrote *The Noble Sport of Warlocks* in 1620, however, the Keeper's job had been simplified. The scoring areas had now been added to the pitch and the Keepers were advised to remain within them, guarding their goal baskets, though Keepers may fly out of this area in an attempt to intimidate opposing Chasers or head them off early.

THE BEATERS

The duties of the Beaters have changed little through the centuries and it is likely that Beaters have existed ever since the introduction of the Bludgers. Their first duty is to guard their team members from the Bludgers, which they do with the aid of bats (once clubs, see Goodwin Kneen's letter in Chapter Three). Beaters have never been goalscorers, nor is there any indication that they have handled the Quaffle.

Beaters need a good deal of physical strength to repel the Bludgers. This is therefore the position that, more than any other, has tended to be taken by wizards rather than witches. Beaters also need to have an excellent sense of balance, as it is sometimes necessary for them to take both hands from their brooms for a double-handed assault on a Bludger.

THE CHASERS

Chaser is the oldest position in Quidditch, for the game once consisted wholly of goalscoring. The Chasers throw the Quaffle to each other and score ten points for every time they get it through one of the goal hoops.

'The Chasers throw the Quaffle to each other and score ten points for every time they get it through one of the goal hoops.'

The only significant change in Chasing came about in 1884, one year after the substitution of goal hoops for goal baskets. A new rule was introduced which stated that only the Chaser carrying the Quaffle could enter the scoring area. If more than one Chaser entered, the goal would be disallowed. The rule was designed to outlaw 'stooging' (see 'Fouls' below), a move by which two Chasers would enter the scoring area and ram the Keeper aside, leaving a goal hoop clear for the third Chaser. Reaction to this new rule was reported in the *Daily Prophet* of the time.

OUR CHASERS AREN'T CHEATING!

DEPARTMENTAL REPRESENTATIVE (BEFORE RETREAT)

BOY CRIES AT STOOGING PENALTY

That was the stunned reaction of Quidditch fans across Britain last night when the so-called 'Stooging Penalty' was announced by the Department of Magical Games and Sports last night.

'Instances of Stooging have been on the increase,' said a harrassed-looking departmental representative last night. 'We feel that this new rule will eliminate the severe Keeper injuries we have been seeing only too often. From now on, one Chaser will attempt to beat the Keeper, as opposed to three Chasers beating the Keeper up. Everything will be much cleaner and fairer.'

At this point the departmental representative was forced to retreat as the angry crowd started to bombard him with Quaffles. Wizards from the Department of Magical Law Enforcement arrived to disperse the crowd, who were threatening to Stooge the Minister for Magic himself.

One freckle-faced six - year - old left the hall in tears.

'I loved Stooging,' he sobbed to the *Daily Prophet*. 'Me and me dad like watching them Keepers flattened. I don't want to go to Quidditch no more.'

Daily Prophet,
22nd June 1884

'Seekers are most likely to be fouled by members of the opposition ... they are usually the players who receive the worst injuries.'

THE SEEKER

Usually the lightest and fastest fliers, Seekers need both a sharp eye and the ability to fly one- or no-handed. Given their immense importance in the overall outcome of the match, for the capture of the Snitch so often snatches victory from the jaws of defeat, Seekers are most likely to be fouled by members of the opposition. Indeed, while there is considerable glamour attached to the position of Seeker, for they are traditionally the best fliers on the pitch, they are usually the players who receive the worst injuries. 'Take out the Seeker' is the first rule in Brutus Scrimgeour's *The Beaters' Bible.*

RULES

The following rules were set down by the Department of Magical Games and Sports upon its formation in 1750:

THE RULES

NO. 1

1. Though there is no limit imposed on the height to which a player may rise during the game, he or she must not stray over the boundary lines of the pitch. Should a player fly over the boundary, his or her team must surrender the Quaffle to the opposing team.

2. The Captain of a team may call for 'time out' by signalling to the referee. This is the only time players' feet are allowed to touch the ground during a match. Time out may be extended to a two-hour period if a game has lasted more than twelve hours. Failure to return to the pitch after two hours leads to the team's disqualification.

THE RULES

NO. 2

THE RULES

NO. 3

3. The referee may award penalties against a team. The Chaser taking the penalty will fly from the central circle towards the scoring area. All players other than the opposing Keeper must keep well back while the penalty is taken.

THE RULES

NO. 4

4. The Quaffle may be taken from another player's grasp but under no circumstances must one player seize hold of any part of another player's anatomy.

5. In the case of injury, no substitution of players will take place. The team will play on without the injured player.

THE RULES

NO. 5

6. Wands may be taken on to the pitch[1] but must under no circumstances whatsoever be used against opposing team members, any opposing team member's broom, the referee, any of the balls or any member of the crowd.

THE RULES

NO. 6

THE RULES

NO. 7

7. A game of Quidditch ends only when the Golden Snitch has been caught, or by mutual consent of the two team Captains.

---

1. The right to carry a wand at all times was established by the International Confederation of Wizards in 1692, when Muggle persecution was at its height and the wizards were planning their retreat into hiding.

FOULS

Rules are of course 'made to be broken'. Seven hundred Quidditch fouls are listed in the Department of Magical Games and Sports records, and all of them are known to have occurred during the final of the first ever World Cup in 1473. The full list of these fouls, however, has never been made available to the wizarding public. It is the Department's view that witches and wizards who see the list 'might get ideas'.

 Department of Magical Games and Sports file containing the full list of Quidditch fouls. This file has never been made public.

I was fortunate enough to gain access to the documents relating to these fouls while researching this book and can confirm that no public good can come of their publication. Ninety per cent of the fouls listed are, in any case, impossible as long as the ban on using wands against the opposing team is upheld (this ban was imposed in 1538). Of the remaining ten per cent, it is safe to say that most would not occur to even the dirtiest player; for example, 'setting fire to an opponent's broom tail', 'attacking an opponent's broom with a club', 'attacking an opponent with an axe'. This is not to say that modern Quidditch players never break rules. Ten common fouls are listed below. The correct Quidditch term for each foul is given in the first column.

NAME	APPLIES TO	DESCRIPTION
Blagging	*All players*	Seizing opponent's broom tail to slow or hinder
Blatching	*All players*	Flying with intent to collide
Blurting	*All players*	Locking broom handles with a view to steering opponent off course
Bumphing	*Beaters only*	Hitting Bludger towards crowd, necessitating a halt of the game as officials rush to protect bystanders. Sometimes used by unscrupulous players to prevent an opposing Chaser scoring
Cobbing	*All players*	Excessive use of elbows towards opponents

Flacking	*Keeper only*	Sticking any portion of anatomy through goal hoop to punch Quaffle out. The Keeper is supposed to block the goal hoop from the front rather than the rear
Haver-sacking	*Chasers only*	Hand still on Quaffle as it goes through goal hoop (Quaffle must be thrown)
Quaffle-pocking	*Chasers only*	Tampering with Quaffle, e.g., puncturing it so that it falls more quickly or zigzags
Snitch-nipping	*All players but Seeker*	Any player other than Seeker touching or catching the Golden Snitch
Stooging	*Chasers only*	More than one Chaser entering the scoring area

72

FOULS

COBBING

FOULS

BLAGGING

FOULS

BUMPHING

FOULS

FLACKING

REFEREES

Refereeing a Quidditch match was once a task for only the bravest witches and wizards. Zacharias Mumps tells us that a Norfolk referee called Cyprian Youdle died during a friendly match between local wizards in 1357. The originator of the curse was never caught but is believed to have been a member of the crowd. While there have been no proven referee slayings since, there have been several incidences of broom-tampering over the centuries, the most dangerous being the transformation of the referee's broom into a Portkey, so that he or she is whisked away from the match halfway through and turns up months later in the Sahara Desert. The Department of Magical Games and Sports has issued strict guidelines on the security measures relating to players' brooms and these incidents are now, thankfully, extremely rare.

Depiction of Norfolk referee Cyprian Youdle being blasted by a mysterious curse during a match in 1357, by artist Vetter Gamily

The effective Quidditch referee needs to be more than an expert flier. He or she has to watch the antics of fourteen players at once and the most common referee's injury is consequently neck strain. At professional matches the referee is assisted by officials who stand around the boundaries of the pitch and ensure that neither players nor balls stray over the outer perimeter.

In Britain, Quidditch referees are selected by the Department of Magical Games and Sports. They have to take rigorous flying tests and an exacting written examination on the rules of Quidditch and prove, through a series of intensive trials, that they will not jinx or curse offensive players even under severe pressure.

CHAPTER SEVEN

Quidditch Teams of Britain and Ireland

QUIDDITCH THROUGH THE AGES

Pride of Portree

Ballycastle Bats

Wigtown Wanderers

Kenmare Kestrels

Falmouth Falcons

Caerphilly Catapults

Montrose Magpies

Appleby Arrows

Holyhead Harpies

Tutshill Tornados

Wimbourne Wasps

76

 Map showing approximate locations of Quidditch Teams of Britain and Ireland

THE NECESSITY FOR KEEPING the game of Quidditch secret from Muggles means that the Department of Magical Games and Sports has had to limit the number of games played each year. While amateur games are permitted as long as the appropriate guidelines are followed, professional Quidditch teams have been limited in number since 1674 when the League was established. At that time, the thirteen best Quidditch teams in Britain and Ireland were selected to join the League and all others were asked to disband. The thirteen teams continue to compete each year for the League Cup.

APPLEBY ARROWS

BALLYCASTLE BATS

CAERPHILLY CATAPULTS

CHUDLEY CANNONS

FALMOUTH
FALCONS

HOLYHEAD HARPIES

78

KENMARE KESTRELS

BRITAIN AND IRELAND

MONTROSE MAGPIES

PRIDE OF PORTREE

PUDDLEMERE
UNITED

TUTSHILL TORNADOS

WIGTOWN WANDERERS

WIMBOURNE
WASPS

TEAM UNIFORMS OF

BALLYCASTLE
BATS

APPLEBY
ARROWS

CAERPHILLY
CATAPULTS

CHUDLEY
CANNONS

HOLYHEAD
HARPIES

FALMOUTH
FALCONS

KENMARE
KESTRELS

BRITAIN AND IRELAND

MONTROSE
MAGPIES

PRIDE OF
PORTREE

PUDDLEMERE
UNITED

TUTSHILL
TORNADOS

WIGTOWN
WANDERERS

WIMBOURNE
WASPS

APPLEBY ARROWS

This northern English team was founded in 1612. Its robes are pale blue, emblazoned with a silver arrow. Arrows fans will agree that their team's most glorious hour was their 1932 defeat of the team who were then the European champions, the Vratsa Vultures, in a match that lasted sixteen days in conditions of dense fog and rain. The club supporters' old practice of shooting arrows into the air from their wands every time their Chasers scored was banned by the Department of Magical Games and Sports in 1894, when

Extract from the
Daily Prophet,
June 1894, with an
illustration depicting
referee Nugent Potts

June 1894

BANNED!

Day 1   Day 2   Day 3   Day 4

Day 5   Day 6   Day 7   Day 8

Day 9   Day 10   Day 11   Day 12

Day 13   Day 14   Day 15   Day 16

 The Appleby Arrows' 1932 defeat of then European champions the Vratsa Vultures, a match that lasted sixteen days in conditions of dense fog and rain one of these weapons pierced the referee, Nugent Potts, through the nose. There is traditionally fierce rivalry between the Arrows and the Wimbourne Wasps (see below).

BALLYCASTLE BATS

Northern Ireland's most celebrated Quidditch team has won the Quidditch League a total of twenty-seven times to date, making it the second most successful in the League's history. The Bats wear black robes with a scarlet bat across the chest. Their famous mascot, Barny the Fruitbat, is also well known as the bat featured in Butterbeer advertisements (*Barny says: I'm just batty about Butterbeer!*).

Beer mat and magazine advertisement featuring Barny the Fruitbat, the Ballycastle Bats' famous mascot (late 20th century)

CAERPHILLY CATAPULTS

The Welsh Catapults, formed in 1402, wear vertically striped robes of light green and scarlet. Their distinguished club history includes eighteen League wins and a famous triumph in the European Cup final of 1956, when they defeated the Norwegian Karasjok Kites. The tragic demise of their most famous player, 'Dangerous Dai' Llewellyn, who was eaten by a Chimaera while on holiday in

'Dangerous Dai' Llewellyn

Caerphilly Catapults

Trading card featuring 'Dangerous Dai' Llewellyn

Postcard sent from 'Dangerous Dai' Llewellyn to his mother the day before he was tragically eaten by a Chimaera whilst on holiday in Mykonos

Mykonos, Greece, resulted in a day of national mourning for all Welsh witches and wizards. The Dangerous Dai Commemorative Medal is now awarded at the end of each season to the League player who has taken the most exciting and foolhardy risks during a game.

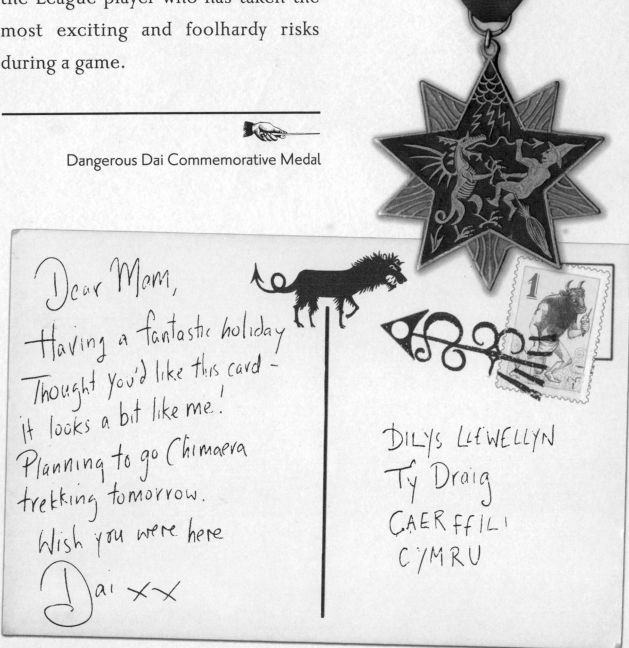

Dangerous Dai Commemorative Medal

Dear Mam,
Having a fantastic holiday
Thought you'd like this card –
it looks a bit like me!
Planning to go Chimaera
trekking tomorrow.
Wish you were here

Dai xx

DILYS LLEWELLYN
Ty Draig
CAERFFILI
CYMRU

CHUDLEY CANNONS

The Chudley Cannons' glory days may be considered by many to be over, but their devoted fans live in hope of a renaissance. The Cannons have won the League twenty-one times, but the last time they did so was in 1892 and their performance over the last century has been lacklustre. The Chudley Cannons wear robes of bright orange emblazoned with a speeding cannonball and a double 'C' in black. The club motto was changed in 1972 from 'We shall conquer' to 'Let's all just keep our fingers crossed and hope for the best'.

'The club motto was changed in 1972 from "We shall conquer"
to "Let's all just keep our fingers crossed and hope for the best".'

 Pre-1972 pin badge and fan T-shirt produced in 1972
after the motto changed

FALMOUTH FALCONS

The Falcons wear dark-grey and white robes with a falcon-head emblem across the chest. The Falcons are known for hard play, a reputation consolidated by their world-famous Beaters, Kevin and Karl Broadmoor, who played for the club from 1958 to 1969 and whose antics resulted in no fewer than fourteen suspensions from the Department of Magical Games and Sports.

Club motto: 'Let us win, but if we cannot win, let us break a few heads.'

Trading cards featuring world-famous Beaters Kevin and Karl Broadmoor (c.1965)

KARL BROADMOOR

KEVIN BROADMOOR

HOLYHEAD HARPIES

The Holyhead Harpies is a very old Welsh club (founded 1203) unique among Quidditch teams around the world because it has only ever hired witches. Harpy robes are dark green with a golden talon upon the chest. The Harpies' defeat of the Heidelberg Harriers in 1953 is widely agreed to have been one of the finest Quidditch games ever seen. Fought over a seven-day period, the game was brought to an end by a spectacular Snitch capture by the Harpy Seeker Glynnis Griffiths. The Harriers' Captain, Rudolf Brand, famously dismounted from his broom at the end of the match and proposed marriage to his opposite number, Gwendolyn Morgan, who concussed him with her Cleansweep Five.

Trading card featuring Harpy Seeker
Glynnis Griffiths (c. 1953)

GLYNNIS GRIFFITHS
(HOLYHEAD HARPIES)

KENMARE KESTRELS

This Irish side was founded in 1291 and is popular worldwide for the spirited displays of their leprechaun mascots and the accomplished harp playing of their supporters. The Kestrels wear emerald-green robes with two yellow 'K's back to back on the chest. Darren O'Hare, Kestrel Keeper 1947–60, captained the Irish national team three times and is credited with the invention of the Chaser Hawkshead Attacking Formation (see Chapter Ten).

KENMARE KESTRELS

Darren O'Hare

Original plan for the Chaser Hawkshead Attacking Formation, on the back of a Butterbeer mat

KENMARE KESTRELS
OFFICIAL
LEPRECHAUN
MASCOT TOY

WARNING: BE CAREFUL WHAT YOU WISH FOR

AUTHENTIC KENMARE KESTRELS ® PRODUCT

94

Kenmare Kestrels
leprechaun toy in
original packaging

MONTROSE MAGPIES

The Magpies are the most successful team in the history of the British and Irish League, which they have won thirty-two times. Twice European champions, the Magpies have fans across the globe. Their many outstanding players include the Seeker Eunice Murray (died 1942), who once petitioned for a

Montrose Magpies in 1938, with Seeker Eunice Murray seated on the far right

'faster Snitch because this is just too easy', and Hamish MacFarlan (Captain 1957–68), who followed his successful Quidditch career with an equally illustrious period as Head of the Department of Magical Games and Sports. The Magpies wear black and white robes with one magpie on the chest and another on the back.

PRIDE OF PORTREE

This team comes from the Isle of Skye, where it was founded in 1292. The 'Prides', as they are known to their fans, wear deep-purple robes with a gold star on the chest. Their most famous Chaser, Catriona McCormack, captained the team to two League wins in the 1960s and played for Scotland thirty-six times. Her daughter Meaghan currently plays Keeper for the team. (Her son Kirley is lead guitarist with the popular wizarding band the Weird Sisters.)

'Catriona McCormack captained the team to two League wins in the 1960s and played for Scotland thirty-six times.'

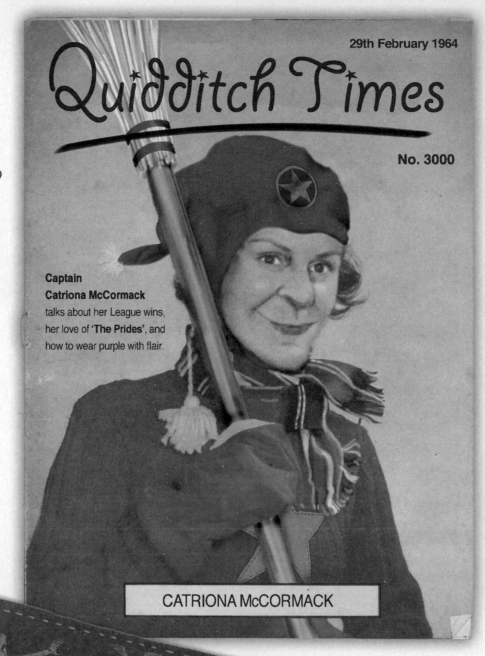

29th February 1964

Quidditch Times

No. 3000

Captain Catriona McCormack talks about her League wins, her love of **'The Prides'**, and how to wear purple with flair.

CATRIONA McCORMACK

97

Pride of Portree pennant and cover of *Quidditch Times*, 29th February 1964

PUDDLEMERE UNITED

Founded in 1163, Puddlemere United is the oldest team in the League. Puddlemere has twenty-two League wins and two European Cup triumphs to its credit. Its team anthem 'Beat Back Those Bludgers, Boys, and Chuck That Quaffle Here' was recently recorded by the singing sorceress Celestina Warbeck to raise funds for St Mungo's Hospital for Magical Maladies and Injuries. Puddlemere players wear navy-blue robes bearing the club emblem of two crossed golden bulrushes.

Charity recording of the Puddlemere United anthem

TUTSHILL TORNADOS

The Tornados wear sky-blue robes with a double 'T' in dark blue on the chest and back. Founded in 1520, the Tornados enjoyed their greatest period of success in the early twentieth century when, captained by Seeker Roderick Plumpton, they won the League Cup five times in a row, a British and Irish record. Roderick Plumpton played Seeker for England twenty-two times and holds the British record for fastest capture of a Snitch during a game (three and a half seconds, against the Caerphilly Catapults, 1921).

Fan memorabilia key ring
(late 20th century)

Photograph of
celebrated Tutshill
Tornado Seeker
Roderick Plumpton
(1907)

'Roderick Plumpton played Seeker for England twenty-two times and
holds the British record for fastest capture of a Snitch during a game
(three and a half seconds, against the Caerphilly Catapults, 1921).'

WIGTOWN WANDERERS

This Borders club was founded in 1422 by the seven offspring of a wizarding butcher named Walter Parkin. The four brothers and three sisters were by all accounts a formidable team who

Illumination depicting the founding members of the Wigtown Wanderers (medieval)

101

rarely lost a match, partly, it is said, because of the intimidation felt by opposing teams at the sight of Walter standing on the sidelines with a wand in one hand and a meat cleaver in the other. A Parkin descendant has often been found on the Wigtown team over the centuries and, in tribute to their origins, the players wear blood-red robes with a silver meat cleaver upon the chest.

WIMBOURNE WASPS

The Wimbourne Wasps wear horizontally striped robes of yellow and black with a wasp upon their chests. Founded in 1312, the Wasps have been eighteen times League winners and twice semi-finalists in the European Cup. They are alleged to have taken their name from a nasty incident

One day when Wimbourne and Appleby did a
game of Quidditch play,
A Wimbourne beater wench did fee
A neft of wafps hung in a tree.
With her club fhe gave the neft a mighty clout,
Out flew the wafps, and laid the Arrows feeker out.

 Printed verse celebrating the Wasps' famous
defeat of the Appleby Arrows (17th century)

which occurred during a match against the Appleby Arrows in the mid-seventeenth century, when a Beater flying past a tree on the edge of the pitch noticed a wasps' nest among the branches and batted it towards the Arrows' Seeker, who was so badly stung that he had to retire from the game. Wimbourne won and thereafter adopted the wasp as their lucky emblem. Wasp fans (also known as 'Stingers') traditionally buzz loudly to distract opposing Chasers when they are taking penalties.

CHAPTER EIGHT

The Spread of
Quidditch Worldwide

EUROPE

 QUIDDITCH WAS WELL ESTABLISHED in Ireland by the fourteenth century, as proved by Zacharias Mumps's account of a match in 1385:

A team of warlocks from Cork flew over for a game in Lancashire and did offend the locals by beating their heroes soundly. The Irishmen knew tricks with the Quaffle that had not been seen in Lancashire before and had to flee the village for fear of their lives when the crowd drew out their wands and gave chase.

 Zacharius Mumps's parchment notebook (1385)

 Illuminated manuscript with the verse written by Ingolfr the Iambic (15th century)

Diverse sources show that the game had spread into other parts of Europe by the early fifteenth century. We know that Norway was an early convert to the game (could Goodwin Kneen's cousin Olaf have introduced the game there?) because of the verse written by the poet Ingolfr the Iambic in the early 1400s:

Oh, the thrill of the chase as I soar through the air
With the Snitch up ahead and the wind in my hair
As I draw ever closer, the crowd gives a shout
But then comes a Bludger and I am knocked out.

Malecrit's play *Hélas, Je me suis Transfiguré Les Pieds* was still being performed four hundred years after it was written, as this poster from Théâtre Magique's 1815 production shows.

Around the same time, the French wizard Malecrit wrote the following lines in his play *Hélas, Je me suis Transfiguré Les Pieds* ('Alas, I've Transfigured My Feet'):

GRENOUILLE: *I cannot go with you to the market today, Crapaud.*
CRAPAUD: *But Grenouille, I cannot carry the cow alone.*
GRENOUILLE: *You know, Crapaud, that I am to be Keeper this morning. Who will stop the Quaffle if I do not?*

'But Grenouille, I cannot carry the cow alone.'
Hélas, Je me suis Transfiguré Les Pieds

The year 1473 saw the first ever Quidditch World Cup, though the nations represented were all European. The nonappearance of teams from more distant nations may be put down to the collapse of owls bearing letters of invitation, the reluctance of those invited to make such a long and perilous journey, or perhaps a simple preference for staying at home.

The final between Transylvania and Flanders has gone down in history as the most violent of all time and many of the fouls then recorded had never been seen before – for instance, the Transfiguration of a Chaser into a polecat, the attempted decapitation of a Keeper with a broadsword

Scenes from the 1473
Quidditch World Cup final by
an unknown Flemish artist,
oil on panel (15th century)

and the release, from under the robes of the Transylvanian Captain, of a hundred blood-sucking vampire bats.

The World Cup has since been held every four years, though it was not until the seventeenth century that non-European teams turned up to compete. In 1652 the European Cup was established, and it has been played every three years since.

Of the many superb European teams, perhaps the Bulgarian **VRATSA VULTURES** is most renowned. Seven times European Cup winners, the Vratsa Vultures are undoubtedly one of the most thrilling teams in the world to watch, pioneers of the long goal (shooting from well outside the scoring area) and always willing to give new players a chance to make a name for themselves.

In France the frequent League winners the **QUIBERON QUAFFLEPUNCHERS** are famed for their flamboyant play as much as for their shocking-pink robes. In Germany we find the **HEIDELBERG HARRIERS**, the team that the Irish Captain Darren O'Hare once famously said was 'fiercer than a dragon and twice as clever'. Luxembourg, always a strong Quidditch nation, has given us the **BIGONVILLE BOMBERS**, celebrated for their offensive strategies and always among the top goalscorers. The Portuguese team **BRAGA BROOMFLEET** have recently broken through into the top levels of the sport with their ground-breaking Beater-marking system; and the Polish **GRODZISK GOBLINS** gave us arguably the world's most innovative Seeker, Josef Wronski.

AUSTRALIA AND NEW ZEALAND

Quidditch was introduced to New Zealand some time in the seventeenth century, allegedly by a team of European herbologists who had gone on an expedition there to research magical plants and fungi. We are told that after a long day's toil collecting samples, these witches and wizards let off steam by playing Quidditch under the bemused gaze of the local magical community. The New Zealand Ministry of Magic has certainly

 Notebook belonging to a European
herbologist (17th century)

spent much time and money preventing Muggles getting hold of Maori art of that period which clearly depicts white wizards playing Quidditch (these carvings and paintings are now on display at the Ministry of Magic in Wellington).

The spread of Quidditch to Australia is believed to have occurred some time in the eighteenth century. Australia may be said to be an ideal Quidditch-playing territory, given the great expanses of uninhabited outback where Quidditch pitches may be established.

Antipodean teams have always thrilled European crowds with their speed and showmanship. Among the best are the **MOUTOHORA MACAWS** (New Zealand), with their famous red, yellow and blue robes

 Maori carving depicting a westerner playing Quidditch,
held by the New Zealand Ministry of Magic (17th century)

and their phoenix mascot, Sparky. The **THUNDELARRA THUNDERERS** and the **WOLLONGONG WARRIORS** have dominated the Australian League for the best part of a century. Their enmity is legendary among the Australian magical community, so much so that a popular response to an unlikely claim or boast is 'Yeah, and I think I'll volunteer to ref the next Thunderer–Warrior game'.

 AFRICA

The broomstick was probably introduced to the African continent by European wizards and witches travelling there in search of information on alchemy and astronomy, subjects in which African wizards have always been particularly skilled. Though not yet as widely played as in Europe, Quidditch is becoming increasingly popular throughout the African continent.

Uganda in particular is emerging as a keen Quidditch-playing nation. Their most notable club, the **PATONGA PROUDSTICKS**, held the Montrose Magpies to a draw in 1986 to the astonishment of most of the Quidditch-playing world. Six Proudstick players recently represented Uganda in the Quidditch World Cup, the highest number of fliers from a single team ever united on a national side. Other African teams of note include the **TCHAMBA CHARMERS** (Togo), masters of the reverse pass; the **GIMBI GIANT-SLAYERS** (Ethiopia), twice winners of the All-Africa Cup; and the **SUMBAWANGA SUNRAYS** (Tanzania), a highly popular team whose formation looping has delighted crowds across the world.

NORTH AMERICA

Quidditch reached the North American continent in the early seventeenth century, although it was slow to take hold there owing to the great intensity of anti-wizarding feeling unfortunately exported from Europe at the same time. The great caution exercised by wizard settlers, many of whom had hoped to find less prejudice in the New World, tended to restrict the growth of the game in its early days.

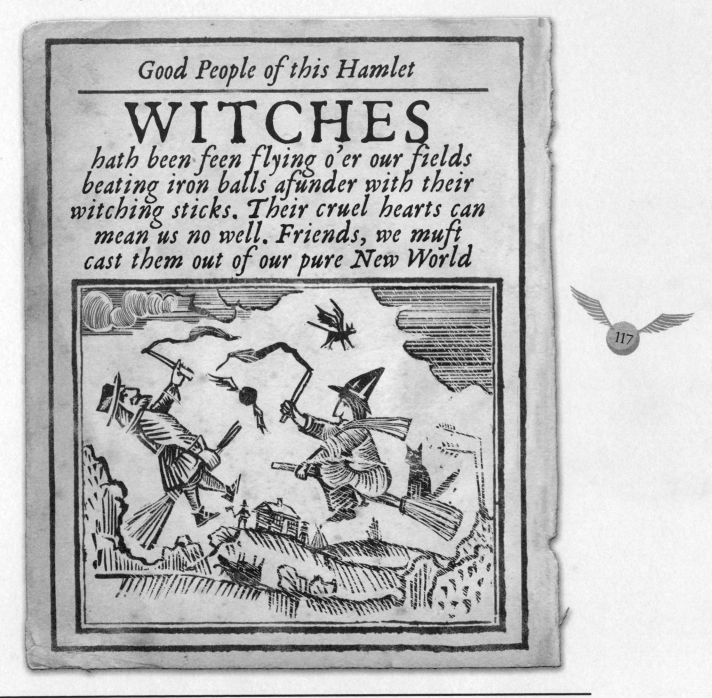

Good People of this Hamlet

WITCHES

hath been feen flying o'er our fields beating iron balls afunder with their witching sticks. Their cruel hearts can mean us no well. Friends, we muft cast them out of our pure New World

117

Pamphlet circulating in the New World circa 1680. Note the failing crops and dying animals, phenomena which were often blamed on the magical community.

In later times, however, Canada has given us three of the most accomplished Quidditch teams in the world: the **MOOSE JAW METEORITES**, the **HAILEYBURY HAMMERS** and the **STONEWALL STORMERS**. The Meteorites were threatened with disbandment in the 1970s owing to their persistent practice of performing post-match victory flights over neighbouring towns and villages while trailing fiery sparks from their broom tails. The team now confines this tradition to the pitch at the end of each match and Meteorite games consequently remain a great wizarding tourist attraction.

The United States has not produced as many world-class Quidditch teams as other nations because the game has had to compete with the American broom game Quodpot. A variant of Quidditch, Quodpot was invented by the eighteenth-century wizard Abraham Peasegood, who had brought a Quaffle with him from the old country and intended to recruit a Quidditch team. The story goes that Peasegood's Quaffle had inadvertently come into contact with the tip of his wand in his trunk, so that when he finally took it out and began to throw it around in a casual manner, it exploded in his face. Peasegood, whose sense of humour appears to have been robust, promptly set out to recreate the effect on a series of leather balls and soon all thought of Quidditch

Promotional poster for the American national Quodpot championship (1946)

was forgotten as he and his friends developed a game which centred on the explosive properties of the newly renamed 'Quod'.

There are eleven players a side in the game of Quodpot. They throw the Quod, or modified Quaffle, from team member to member, attempting to get it into the 'pot' at the end of the pitch before it explodes. Any player in possession of the Quod when it explodes must leave the pitch. Once the Quod is safely in the 'pot' (a small cauldron containing a solution which will prevent the Quod exploding), the scorer's team is awarded a point and a new Quod is brought on to the pitch. Quodpot has had some success as a minority sport in Europe, though the vast majority of wizards remain faithful to Quidditch.

The rival charms of Quodpot notwithstanding, Quidditch is gaining popularity in the United States. Two teams have recently broken through at international level: the **Sweetwater All-Stars** from Texas, who gained a well-deserved win over the Quiberon Quafflepunchers in 1993 after a thrilling five-day match; and the **Fitchburg Finches** from Massachusetts, who have now won the US League seven times and whose Seeker, Maximus Brankovitch III, has captained America at the last two World Cups.

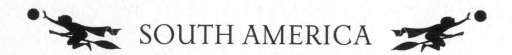

SOUTH AMERICA

Quidditch is played throughout South America, though the game must compete with the popular Quodpot here as in the North. Argentina and Brazil both reached the quarter-finals of the World Cup in the last century. Undoubtedly the most skilled Quidditch nation in South America is Peru, which is tipped to become the first Latin World Cup winner within ten years. Peruvian warlocks are believed to have had their first exposure to Quidditch from European wizards sent by the International Confederation to monitor the numbers of Vipertooths (Peru's native dragon). Quidditch has become a veritable obsession of the wizard community there since that time, and their most famous team, the **Tarapoto Tree-Skimmers**, recently toured Europe to great acclaim.

ASIA

Quidditch has never achieved great popularity in the East, as the flying broomstick is a rarity in countries where the carpet is still the preferred mode of travel. The Ministries of Magic in countries such as

 This rare Japanese plate is thought to date from the late nineteenth century and depicts Japanese witches and wizards on a Quidditch pitch. It was found in a pile of discarded pottery on the outskirts of Toyohashi and was obviously rejected due to its low quality. It is assumed to be the work of an apprentice.

Woodblock print depicting Lithuania's Gorodok
Gargoyles' win over the Toyohashi Tengu in 1994

負けた

India, Pakistan, Bangladesh, Iran and Mongolia, all of whom maintain a flourishing trade in flying carpets, regard Quidditch with some suspicion, though the sport does have some fans among witches and wizards on the street.

The exception to this general rule is Japan, where Quidditch has been gaining steadily in popularity over the last century. The most successful Japanese team, the **TOYOHASHI TENGU**, narrowly missed a win over Lithuania's Gorodok Gargoyles in 1994. The Japanese practice of ceremonially setting fire to their brooms in case of defeat is, however, frowned upon by the International Confederation of Wizards' Quidditch Committee as being a waste of good wood.

CHAPTER NINE

The Development of the
Racing Broom

NTIL THE EARLY NINETEENTH century, Quidditch was played on day brooms of varying quality. These brooms represented a massive advance over their medieval forerunners; the invention of the Cushioning Charm by Elliot Smethwyck in 1820 went a long way towards making broomsticks more comfortable than ever before (see Fig. F opposite). Nevertheless, nineteenth-century broomsticks were generally incapable of achieving high speeds and were often difficult to control at high altitudes. Brooms tended to be hand-produced by individual broom-makers and while they are admirable from the point of view of styling and craftsmanship, their performance rarely matched up to their handsome appearance.

A case in point is the **OAKSHAFT 79** (so named because the first example was created in 1879). Crafted by the broom-maker Elias Grimstone of Portsmouth, the Oakshaft is a handsome broom with a very thick oaken

Oakshaft 79

COMFORT BROOM

The *Comfort Broom™* is by far the most comfortable broom on sale today, and it doesn't rely on any fancy-schmancy cushioning charm to provide top class comfort (unlike some others).

AVAILABLE IN A RANGE OF FABRICS

Contact B. Fanadl by owl for more details

Not suitable for use in high winds, at speed, or in rainy conditions

⚜ Broom Buddy ⚜

Made by hand in Ireland
For details and a chance to fly before you buy
Send an owl to Saoirse Scuab

BELL'S BROOMS
THE WORLDS MOST BEAUTIFUL BROOMS

Make your next broom a *BOOM BROOM*
The Dynamic new shape provides more stability when carrying uneven loads.

Owls to B. Tsotskhi

ELLIOT SMETHWYCK'S WORLD FAMOUS CUSHIONING CHARM

Works like a CHARM!

A hard broom makes even the shortest of flights a pain in the rear. Leave that pain behind with Elliot Smethwyck's world famous patented CUSHIONING CHARM™. Suitable for all makes of magical brooms.

In a survey

99% of witches and warlocks agreed that "Riding a broom treated with Elliot Smethwyck's world famous patented CUSHIONING CHARM is just like floating on a feather bed!"

99% of 37 Witches and Warlocks

Smethwyck's CUSHIONING CHARM

JUST ONE OF THE *CHARMS IN A TUBE™* RANGE

TGA CC233

What-ever the weather Day or night

Brush it off when you fly on a **'BOB'S SUPER LIGHT'!**

Guaranteed to keep you dry and visible in inclement conditions

★ ★ ★ ★

(Guaranteed only to speeds of under 10mph, and heights of 5 metres)

Fig. F Elliot Smethwyck's Cushioning Charm, from Classified section of WHICH BROOMSTICK?, January 1821

handle, designed for endurance flying and to withstand high winds. The Oakshaft is now a highly prized vintage broom, but attempts to use it for Quidditch were never successful. Too cumbersome to turn at high speed, the Oakshaft never gained much popularity with those who prized agility over safety, though it will always be remembered as the broom used in the first ever Atlantic broom crossing, by Jocunda Sykes in 1935. (Before that time, wizards preferred to take ships rather than trust broomsticks over such distances. Apparition becomes increasingly unreliable over very long distances, and only highly skilled wizards are wise to attempt it across continents.)

'The Oakshaft ... will always be remembered as the broom used in the first ever Atlantic broom crossing, by Jocunda Sykes in 1935.'

Signed fan photograph of Jocunda Sykes, circa 1935

The **MOONTRIMMER**, which was first created by Gladys Boothby in 1901, represented a leap forward in broom construction, and for a while

Moontrimmer

these slender, ash-handled brooms were in great demand as Quidditch brooms. The Moontrimmer's principal advantage over other brooms was its ability to achieve greater heights than ever before (and remain controllable at such altitudes). Gladys Boothby was unable to produce Moontrimmers in the quantities Quidditch players clamoured for. The production of a new broom, the **SILVER ARROW**, was welcomed; this was the true forerunner of the racing broom, achieving much higher

Moontrimmer advertising flyer (1901)

speeds than the Moontrimmer or Oakshaft (up to seventy miles an hour with a tailwind), but like these it was the work of a single wizard (Leonard Jewkes) and demand far outstripped supply.

Silver Arrow

The breakthrough occurred in 1926, when the brothers Bob, Bill and Barnaby Ollerton started the Cleansweep Broom Company. Their first model, the **Cleansweep One**, was produced in numbers never seen

 Photograph of the Ollerton brothers, founders of the Cleansweep Broom Company

before and marketed as a racing broom specifically designed for sporting use. The Cleansweep was an instant, runaway success, cornering as no broom before it, and within a year, every Quidditch team in the country was mounted on Cleansweeps.

Cleansweep One

The Ollerton brothers were not left in sole possession of the racing-broom market for long. In 1929 a second racing-broom company was established by Randolph Keitch and Basil Horton, both players for the Falmouth Falcons. The Comet Trading Company's first broom was the **Comet 140**, this being the number of models that Keitch and Horton

Comet 140

had tested prior to its release. The patented Horton–Keitch braking charm meant that Quidditch players were much less likely to overshoot goals or fly offside, and the Comet now became the broom of preference for many British and Irish teams in consequence.

While the Cleansweep–Comet competition became more intense, marked by the release of the improved Cleansweeps Two and Three in 1934 and 1937 respectively, and the Comet 180 in 1938, other broomstick manufacturers were springing up all over Europe.

Cleansweep Two

Cleansweep Three

Comet 180

The **TINDERBLAST** was launched on the market in 1940. Produced by the Black Forest company Ellerby and Spudmore, the Tinderblast is a highly resilient broom, though it has never achieved the top speeds of the Comets and Cleansweeps. In 1952 Ellerby and Spudmore brought

Tinderblast

out a new model, the **SWIFTSTICK**. Faster than the Tinderblast, the Swiftstick nevertheless has a tendency to lose power in ascent and has never been used by professional Quidditch teams.

Swiftstick

In 1955 Universal Brooms Ltd introduced the **SHOOTING STAR**, the cheapest racing broom to date. Unfortunately, after its initial burst of popularity, the Shooting Star was found to lose speed and height as it aged, and Universal Brooms went out of business in 1978.

Shooting Star

In 1967 the broom world was galvanised by the formation of the Nimbus Racing Broom Company. Nothing like the **NIMBUS 1000**

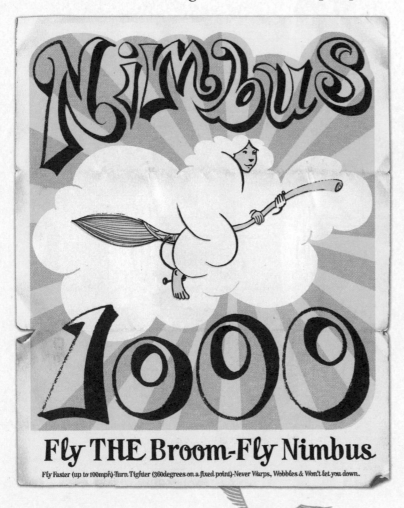

had ever been seen before. Reaching speeds of up to a hundred miles per hour, capable of turning 360 degrees at a fixed point in mid-air, the Nimbus combined the reliability of the old Oakshaft 79 with the easy handling of the best Cleansweeps. The Nimbus immediately became the broom preferred by professional

Promotional advertisement for the Nimbus 1000 (1967)

Nimbus 1000
Fly THE Broom-Fly Nimbus
Fly Faster (up to 100mph)-Turn Tighter (360degrees on a fixed point)-Never Warps, Wobbles & Won't let you down.

Quidditch teams across Europe, and the subsequent models (1001, 1500 and 1700) have kept the Nimbus Racing Broom Company at the top of the field.

Nimbus 1000

The **TWIGGER 90**, first produced in 1990, was intended by its manufacturers, Flyte and Barker, to replace the Nimbus as market leader. However, though highly finished and including a number of new gimmicks such as an inbuilt Warning Whistle and Self-Straightening Brush, the Twigger has been found to warp under high speeds and has gained the unlucky reputation of being flown by wizards with more Galleons than sense.

Twigger 90

CHAPTER TEN

Quidditch Today

THE GAME OF QUIDDITCH continues to thrill and obsess its many fans around the world. Nowadays every purchaser of a Quidditch match ticket is guaranteed to witness a sophisticated contest between highly skilled fliers (unless of course the Snitch is caught in the first five minutes of the match, in which case we all feel slightly short-changed). Nothing demonstrates this more than the difficult moves that have been invented over its long history by witches and wizards eager to push themselves and the game as far as they can go. Some of these are listed below.

Official tickets to international and local fixtures are highly prized collectables.

Bludger Backbeat

A move by which the Beater strikes the Bludger with a backhanded club swing, sending it behind him or her rather than in front. Difficult to bring off with precision but excellent for confusing opponents.

Dopplebeater Defence

Both Beaters hit a Bludger at the same time for extra power, resulting in a Bludger attack of greater severity.

Double-Eight Loop

A Keeper defence, usually employed against penalty takers, whereby the Keeper swerves around all three goal hoops at high speed to block the Quaffle.

Hawkshead Attacking Formation

Chasers form an arrowhead pattern and fly together towards the goalposts. Highly intimidating to opposing teams and effective in forcing other players aside.

PARKIN'S PINCER

Parkin's Pincer

So named for the original members of the Wigtown Wanderers, who are reputed to have invented this move. Two Chasers close in on an opposing Chaser on either side, while the third flies headlong towards him or her.

Plumpton Pass

Seeker move: a seemingly careless swerve that scoops the Snitch up one's sleeve. Named after Roderick Plumpton, Tutshill Tornado Seeker, who employed the move in his famous record-breaking Snitch catch of 1921. Although some critics have alleged that this was an accident, Plumpton maintained until his death that he had meant to do it.

PLUMPTON PASS

PORSKOFF PLOY

Porskoff Ploy

The Chaser carrying the Quaffle flies upwards, leading opposing Chasers to believe he or she is trying to escape them to score, but then throws the Quaffle downwards to a fellow Chaser waiting to catch it. Pinpoint timing is of the essence. Named after the Russian Chaser Petrova Porskoff.

Reverse Pass

A Chaser throws the Quaffle over one shoulder to a team member. Accuracy is difficult.

REVERSE PASS

Sloth Grip Roll

Hanging upside down off the broom, gripping tightly with hands and feet to avoid a Bludger.

SLOTH GRIP ROLL

FIG. G

STARFISH AND STICK

Starfish and Stick

Keeper defence: the Keeper holds the broom horizontally with one hand and one foot curled around the handle, while keeping all limbs outstretched (see Fig. G). The Starfish without Stick should never be attempted.

Transylvanian Tackle

First seen at the World Cup of 1473, this is a fake punch aimed at the nose. As long as contact is not made, the move is not illegal, though it is difficult to pull off when both parties are on speeding broomsticks.

TRANSYLVANIAN TACKLE

WOLLONGONG SHIMMY

Wollongong Shimmy

Perfected by the Australian Wollongong Warriors, this is a high-speed zig-zagging movement intended to throw off opposing Chasers.

Wronski Feint

The Seeker hurtles towards the ground pretending to have seen the Snitch far below, but pulls out of the dive just before hitting the pitch. Intended to make the opposing Seeker copy him and crash. Named after the Polish Seeker Josef Wronski.

WRONSKI FEINT

THERE CAN BE NO doubt that Quidditch has changed beyond
all recognition since Gertie Keddle first watched 'those numbskulls'
on Queerditch Marsh. Perhaps, had she lived today, she too would
have thrilled to the poetry and power of Quidditch. Long may the
game continue to evolve and long may future generations of
witches and wizards enjoy this most glorious of sports!

J.K. ROWLING

J.K. ROWLING is best known as the author of the seven Harry Potter books, which were published between 1997 and 2007. The enduringly popular adventures of Harry, Ron and Hermione have gone on to sell over 500 million copies, be translated into over 80 languages and made into eight blockbuster films. Alongside the Harry Potter series, she also wrote three short companion volumes for charity: *Quidditch Through the Ages* and *Fantastic Beasts and Where to Find Them*, in aid of Comic Relief and Lumos, and *The Tales of Beedle the Bard*, in aid of Lumos. J.K. Rowling collaborated with playwright Jack Thorne and director John Tiffany to continue Harry's story in a stage play, *Harry Potter and the Cursed Child*, which opened in London in 2016 and is now playing in Europe, North America and Australia. In the same year, she made her debut as a screenwriter with the film *Fantastic Beasts and Where to Find Them*, the first in a series featuring Magizoologist Newt Scamander, which was inspired by the original companion volume. J.K. Rowling has also written a standalone novel, *The Casual Vacancy*, and is the author of the Strike crime series under the pseudonym Robert Galbraith. Both have been adapted for television. She has received many awards and honours, including an OBE and a Companion of Honour for services to literature and philanthropy. She lives in Scotland with her family.

EMILY GRAVETT

EMILY GRAVETT is the author and illustrator of many award-winning children's books. After leaving school with few qualifications, she spent eight years living on the road before taking the BA Illustration course at Brighton University. She won the Macmillan Prize for Illustration with her first book, *Wolves*, which went on to win the Kate Greenaway Medal and the Boston Globe Horn Book Honor Award for Illustration and marked the beginning of an international career creating extraordinary and innovative books for children: *Little Mouse's Big Book of Fears* won the Kate Greenaway Medal for her a second time. In 2019 she was crowned the winner of the first ever BookTrust Storytime Prize for her picture book *Cyril and Pat*. Her own picture books are published in more than 20 languages and she has also collaborated with some of the most creative writers working today, including Julia Donaldson, A.F. Harrold and Matt Haig. Emily lives in Brighton with her partner and a dog called Dilys.

COMIC RELIEF

Since 2001, *Quidditch Through the Ages* and *Fantastic Beasts and Where to Find Them* have raised nearly £20 million for Comic Relief – a magic amount of money that is already hard at work changing lives.

Money raised through the sale of this new edition will be invested in children and young people around the world, preparing them to be ready for the future – to be safe, healthy, educated and empowered. We are particularly interested in helping those children who start their lives in the most difficult circumstances, where there is conflict, violence, neglect or abuse.

Thank you for your support. To find out more about Comic Relief go to comicrelief.com, follow us on Twitter (@comicrelief) or like us on Facebook!

LUMOS
Protecting Children. Providing Solutions.

There are eight million children living in orphanages worldwide – even though eighty per cent of them are not orphans.

Most children are institutionalised because their parents are poor and cannot adequately provide for them. And while many institutions are established or supported with good intentions, more than eighty years of research proves that raising children in orphanages harms their health and development, increases their exposure to abuse and trafficking and seriously reduces their chances of a happy, healthy future.

Put simply, children need families, not orphanages.

Lumos, a charity founded by J.K. Rowling, is named after the light-giving spell from Harry Potter that brings light to the darkest of places. At Lumos that is exactly what we do. We reveal the children hidden away in institutions and transform systems of care globally so that all children have the families they need and the futures they deserve.

Thank you for buying this book. If you would like to join J.K. Rowling and Lumos as part of our global movement for change you can find out how to get involved at wearelumos.org, @lumos and Facebook.